Biography of the founder of religion (of all religions)

Abdul Waheed

Biography of the founder of religion (of all religions)

Abdul Waheed

© **Abdul Waheed**

No copying of this book with out permission

Dedication

This book is dedicated to the memory of my late father Haji Ubairdur Rahman (Munna) and younger brother Abdul Hameed. May God (Allah) give peace to his soul.

Aamen

Table of contents

Preface

In this presentation, the life introduction of the originator or founder of almost all major religions of the world has been explained in detail. The life introduction of the founder of any religion is important because if you do not know about the life of the founder, then it will not be easy to understand that religion too, so it is my effort to tell about the life introduction so that you can get information if If you see any deficiency, inform immediately, if the subject seems less, then give information,
thanks .
Yours Abdul Waheed, Barabanki, UP, India.

Life introduction of Mohammad Sahab (SA)-(Islam religion)

Mohammad Sahib (s 0) was born in a city called Mecca in Arabia. His father's name was Abdullah and mother's name was Amina, his grandfather's name was "Abu Muttalib". Father died before his birth. His dynasty was famous as 'Hasim dynasty'. When Hazrat Mohammad was only 6 years old. When his mother died, he became an orphan at a very young age (Sur. 936). His grandfather Abdul Muttalib took the responsibility of his upbringing on his shoulders, but Hazrat Mohammad was only 8 years old. His grandfather also died. Then his uncle Hazrat Abu Talib (father of Hazrat Ali) became his guardian. At the age of 12, he went on his first trip to Syria with his uncle, in this journey he met a Christian monk named Bahira. Seeing him, it was prophesied that he would get a superior position. When he was 15 years old, he also participated in a war and in that he did the work of choosing the arrows of the enemy and giving them to his comrades, Hazrat Mohammad because of his honesty among all was recognized and called Al-Amin. Your childhood was spent in the lap of a Badawi nurse, according to the custom of the time, which was the language of Banu Sa'd Taksali was spoken. When you turned 25, your uncle got you a job in 515 AD with Hazrat Khadija, a well-respected widow of the Quraysh clan. Khadija was skilled in business and was a prosperous woman. Impressed by the behavior and honesty of Hazrat Mohammad, he sent Hazrat Mohammad as the head of his trade convoy towards Syria. You ended this business trip very efficiently and on his safe return from the trip to Syria, Khadija was very happy and requested him to marry her, which you gladly accepted. Hazrat Khadija was 40 years old at the time of marriage. Hazrat Mo.'s married life with you was very happy. Khadija had two sons and four daughters. But except for Hazrat Fatima who was the wife of Ali and also the mother of Hasan and Hussain, all the children died during his (Prophet's) lifetime.

There are the following differences regarding the date of birth of the Prophet:

1- Hazrat Mo was born on 29 August 570 AD (Arab Culture Part 1)

2 Hazrat born 20 April 570 AD (An Introduction to Islam, New Edition)

3 Hazrat Mo 0 was born on April 22, 571 AD (Prophet of Islam God have mercy on him)

It became the nature of Hazrat Mohammad to pray to God in the cave of Hira. From the very beginning, he had hatred for idol worship. At the age of 41 (609 AD), he received a call from God.

After this he was fully convinced that God had chosen him for the throne. When Hazrat Muhammad (pbuh) started presenting the message of Allah to the people of Mecca as a preacher, the first impact of his message was on his wife. After that Hazrat Zaid and Hazrat Ali agreed with his views. In this way, within three years, about fifty persons accepted Islam. This group of Muslims hated idol worship and tried wholeheartedly that the people of Mecca should give up idol worship and become worshipers of one Allah. But those who have traditional religious beliefs found his words meaningless and that is why many people became his enemies. In the end, the situation became so critical that on 20 June 622 AD, he had to leave Mecca and take refuge in Medina. This incident is famous in the history of Islam by the name of Hijrat. Some scholars consider this incident on 16 July 622 AD. Hazrat Mohammad S 0 declared that God is one and Mohammad is the Nabi or Prophet of that God. The Holy Qur'an is a splendid proof of all these teachings.

The number of wives of Hazrat Mohammad is said to be 11.

(1) Khadija, (2) Widow of Sakran, old woman Sauda' daughter Jama (3) Ayesha daughter of Hazrat Abu Bakr (4) Hafsah daughter of Umar bin Khattab, (5) Zainab daughter of Khazima Razi. (6) Umme Kulsum Hind daughter of Amiya Razi 0 (7) Zainab Patri Wa

Jahsh bin Riyab (8) Juwairiya daughter of Haris, (9) Umme Hawibah daughter of Abu Sufiyan, (10) Safiyeh daughter of Hayyabin (II) Maimunah Quresh Dar Haris (12)) Maria Kibatia (13) Rehana daughter of Zaid Ruqaiya o
Hazrat Mohammad Sallallahu Alaihi Wasallam had 4 daughters.

(1) Hazrat Zainab (2) Fatima (R.A.) (3) Ruqaiya (4) Umme Kulsoom, Hazrat Zainab, the eldest daughter of Hazrat Mohammad Sallallahu Alaihi Sallam, who was the wife of Hazrat Aas and Hazrat Abul Aas was the son-in-law of Hazrat Muhammad Sahib. Hazrat Fatima was married to Hazrat Ali, who was also the son-in-law of Hazrat Muhammad. Hazrat Muhammad SAW has said that Hazrat Fatima will be the leader of women in Jannah. Hazrat Ruqaiya who was in the marriage of Hazrat Usman, after Ruqaiya, Hazrat Umm Kulsoom came in the marriage of Hazrat Usman. Hazrat Usman was also the son-in-law of Hazrat Mohammad. From Hijrat, the family of the Prophet in Mecca was united with you and your wife Hazrat Khadija. At the time of marriage, you were 25 years old and Hazrat Khadija Razi 0 was 40 years old. Hazrat Khadija was the first wife and you did not marry anyone else while she was alive. In your progeny, apart from Hazrat Ibrahim, all the sons and daughters-in-law were from the body of this Hazrat Khadija; Their names are Zainab Ruqayya Razi, Umm Kulsoom Razi 0 and Fatima Razi 0. Zainab was married to her cousin Abul Aas bin Rabia before

Hijrat. Ruqya and Umm Kulsoom were married one after the other to Hazrat Usman. Hazrat Fatima was married to Hazrat Ali bin Abu Talib in the middle of Jag Badr and Jang Ahand, and Hazrat Muhammad (S.A.) had a life full of enjoyment and luxury from whom Hasan Hussain and Umm Kulsoom were born. It will be known from the sentence in which it has been said that the prophet should tell his women if you want worldly life and its pleasures, then come and give you something and send you well. God has fixed the best result for such virtuous women. (33:4:1,2)

Although you did not lack wealth. Nevertheless, you considered the simple life of fasting and the life of a beggar to be the best. Despite being a servant, he used to like to do his own work. Treating the slaves with equality, treating the poor and the poor with humility and kindness was a great quality of yours. No beggar or fakir or traveler used to return disappointed from your door. You were generous by nature and truthful in your words. Never used to take out any bad thing from his tongue. He used to spend more and more time in the discussion of Allah and in Namaz. He used to fast regularly. Despite this, he used to extend his hand in household chores. They used to try to give every kind of happiness to their wives and fulfill their every need. He used to love children and seeing them happy, he himself was also happy. The gifts that used to come were distributed among the poor, Miraj to Hazrat Mohammad. Nishapatra) related to Krandan Diwan (Walling Wall) is a belief among Muslims that he was Buraq. It was from here that he flew towards the sky carrying Hazrat Mohammad No. Two years after this amazing visit, a group of seventy-five persons invited Hazrat Muhammad to come and stay in Mecca. The Jews in Medina were looking forward to the coming of a Messiah and had prepared their pagan inhabitants to welcome him. Three years after his return to Madinah, he suddenly fell ill and died. You had severe headache. This incident happened on June 8, 632 AD.

According to the statement of Hazrat Mohammad S. 0, Hazrat Mohammad S. 0 loved three things

(1) Women (2) Fragrance (3) Delicious food in which sweet chicks were more loved. It was dear to eat dates mixed with honey. He disliked silk clothes and kept long hair on his head. They used to take out demand by pouring oil from time to time. He used to apply antimony to his eyes and also used to teach others to apply antimony. Your beard had grown and the mustache was thin and non-existent. Your complexion was fair and your body was strong. The shoulders were broad. You were tall, had a slight smile on your face and used to treat everyone with civility while talking. Used to listen to everyone's words very carefully. He used to answer each and every question appropriately and concisely. There was control over anger and habit of walking fast. Always ask Allah for forgiveness for your weaknesses and errors and pray that even after all I am a human

being, if I have hurt anyone, then O Allah, forgive me. Never used to lose courage, used to thank Allah in sorrow and trouble. You were called a magician poet, Majnu, you were insulted. Dirt, stones and thorns were thrown in your way but you tolerated all these with patience. History is witness to the fact that even your enemies did not accuse you of telling falsehood or doing any other heinous act. According to Hazrat Ayesha, you were the Quran incarnate. All the virtues were present in you. He used to go to the mosque regularly, wherever he got a place, he used to sit here among the people. Never wished to sit at a particular place, according to Hazrat Muhammad SAW, all human beings are equal in the eyes of God, no one is superior to the other on the basis of color and caste.

Miracles of Hazrat Mohammad

(1) When you threw it, you did not throw it, God threw it. 2:218 At the time of the Battle of Badr, Hazrat Muhammad had thrown a handful of soil towards the enemies. Due to this the enemy was defeated. 2) The hour approached when the moon was split (51:1:1). This is the description of the miracle called Shakkulaksar of Hazrat. To show his divine power, Hazrat once pointed his finger towards the moon, on which it broke into two pieces. Which was seen by many of his followers. Hazrat Mohammad did not claim to have laid the foundation of any new religion, he propagated the

same Deen Deen Ibrahim or the cult of Ibrahim, which existed thousands of years before Hazrat Mohammad.

Tafsir of holy Quran
Surah Al Ahjaab 33, verse 21

Abu Bakr al-Jazairi (born 1921 AD)
Asr al-Tafsir's interpretation of the words of Abu Bakr al-Jazairi (d. 2018 AD).

Word Explanation:

They understand the parties: that is, they are cowardly hypocrites who think that the parties are the Quraysh and the Ghatafan.

They did not go, that is, they did not return to their country disappointed.

And if parties come: that, again, is mandatory.

They wish they were in the desert among the Bedouins: that is, because of their cowardice and fear, they wish they were in the desert with its inhabitants.

They ask your news: that is, if they were there at the beginning, if the parties return, they ask your news, that is, whether you lost or won.

If they had been among you, they would not have fought except a few. That is, if they had been among you in the city, they would not have fought you except a few.

A good role model: i.e. a good role model that you can follow, may God bless him and grant him peace in his fight and perseverance in his country.

This is what God and His angel promised us: trial and victory.

And God and His messenger were true to their promise.

This only increased their faith and submission: that is, faith in God's promise and submission to God's command.

They were true to what they promised God: that is, they kept their promise.

Some of them kept their vow and continued fighting until they were martyred.

Some of them are waiting: that is, they are still fighting the battle with the messenger of God, waiting to be killed for God.

And they changed nothing: that is, in their covenant, they broke their covenant, unlike the hypocrites.God restored the unbelievers because of their anger: that is, God restored the sorrows. The context is still in narrating the events of the Battle of Al-Ahzab, as God Almighty says, "They think that the parties Haven't gone." That is, they think that they are hypocritical cowards who said that our houses are shameful and said to their brothers, "Come to us." That is, leave Muhammad alone in the foreground. Because of their cowardice, they thought that the parties have not returned to their country despite having gone, and this is extreme cowardice and fear, and the saying of the Almighty {and if the parties come} again on the basis of meaning, perception and order { They wish} that day {that they were alone among the Bedouins} meaning their intense fear of the raiding parties in the desert with the Bedouins outside the city and for the saying of their Almighty {He asks and about your news} I mean, do you have any news? whether the parties conquered you or not, {and if they were among you} among you and not in the desert {they would not have fought you except a little} and this is due to their cowardice and belief in the advantage of fighting The lack is because of their disbelief in meeting

Almighty God and in His reward and punishment. This is what is included in the first verse [20].

And God Almighty says in the second verse [21] {Indeed there is a good example for you in the Messenger of God who has hope in God and the Last Day and remembers God often} which means: He has given you a .

Surah Al Qalam 68 verse 4

Tafsir Abu Bakr al-Jazairi (born 1921 AD)

Asr al-Tafsir's interpretation of the words of Abu Bakr al-Jazairi (d. 2018 AD).

Word Explanation:
NEV: This is one of the disjointed letters, written like NEV and read as NUN.

And the pen and what they write: that is, the pen with which remembrance, "destiny" is written and with which they write and write.

You are not by the grace of your Lord: that is, you are not because of the providence that God gave you and the perfection that He gave you.

Mad: That is, mad, as the polytheists claim.

Ungrateful: That is, it is not interrupted, but it is eternal.

Which of you is fascinated? Which means which one of you is crazy?

Tafsir Ibne Kasir

Sura Al Kalam 68, verse 4

And indeed, you are on a higher character.

Al-Awfi reported from Ibn Abbas,

"Indeed, you are upon a great religion, and it is Islam."

Similarly, Mujahid, Abu Malik, As-Suddi and Ar-Rabi bin Anas also said. Ad-Dahhak and Ibn Zayd also said this.

Sa'id bin Abi 'Aruba narrated from Qatada that he said regarding the statement of Allah,

and (And in fact, you are at a higher (standard) character).

"We are told that when Sa'd bin Hisham asked A'isha about the character of the Messenger of Allah, she replied:

'Haven't you read the Quran?'

Saad said: 'Of course.'
Then he said: 'Verily, the character of the Messenger of Allah was the Quran."

 Abdur-Razzaq recorded similar to this and Imam Muslim recorded it in its full length in his Sahih on the authority of Qatada.

This means that he will act in accordance with the commands and prohibitions given in the Quran. Their disposition and character were shaped by the Quran, and they abandoned their natural nature (i.e., physical disposition). Therefore, whatever the Quran ordered, he did, and whatever was forbidden, he abstained from.

Along with this, Allah also gave him noble character, which included humility, kindness, bravery, forgiveness, humility and all other good qualities. This is as confirmed by Anas in two Sahih,

"I served the Messenger of Allah for ten years, and he never said a word of displeasure to me (oops), nor did he ever say to me about any of my deeds: 'Why did you do this?'"

And he never asked me about the work which I did not do, why did you not do it.

He had the best character, and I never touched silk or anything else that was softer than the palm of the Messenger of Allah. And I have never smelled any musk or perfume whose fragrance is better than the sweat of the Messenger of Allah."

Imam al-Bukhari recorded that al-Bara said,

"The face of the Messenger of Allah was the most beautiful of all people, and his manners were the best of all people. And he was neither tall, nor was he short."

The hadiths related to this matter are numerous. Abu Isa at-Tirmidhi has an entire book on this subject called Kitab ash-Shamā'il.

Imam Ahmad recorded that Aisha said,
The Messenger of Allah never hit his servant with his hand, nor did he ever hit a woman. He never hit anything with his hand, except when he was fighting Jihad for Allah."

And he was never given a choice between two things, except that which of the two he loved most, was the easiest, unless it involved sin. If it involved sin, he abstained from sin more than any other man.

He will not take revenge for anything done to him, except that which transgressed the limits of Allah. Then, in that case he will take revenge for the sake of Allah."

Imam Ahmad also recorded from Abu Huraira that the Messenger of Allah said,

إِنَّمَا بُعِثْتُ لِأُتَمِّمَ سَالِحَ الأُكْلَق

I have been sent only for perfect religious conduct.

Ahmad was alone in recording this hadith.

Introduction to the life of Jesus Christ (Hazrat Isa (A)(Christianity)

Hazrat Isa was born from the womb of the virgin Mary, estimated at 4 BC in an inn in the city of Bechelham in Judea (Judaia) province. Was born in a cowshed. Jesus Christ or Jesus Christ was a Jew. Authentic description of his life is not available. It is definitely known on the basis of Bible and New Testament that since childhood, Jesus was interested in commentaries of religious texts. And Bhagya was in reading. He also took special interest in the study of theology. The curiosity to attain truth and understand God was in his heart from a very young age, taking the opportunity he would go to the forest, talk to scholars and religious When Jesus grew up, he learned the profession of his father Joseph and lived in the same village until the age of 30. He continued to work as a carpenter. Later, he left this work and started fulfilling his purpose. The event was a meeting with John in 27 A.D. John was a Jew and lived on the banks of the Jordan River.It was from here that his spiritual life began. , For forty days he stayed in the Judaean desert.

People believed that the desert is inhabited by ghosts and evil spirits. When Jesus was there, people started saying many kinds of things. He had a fierce struggle with the devil. At last, after overcoming many temptations and doing severe penance for 40 days, he realized himself.

Jesus said that sin is ruling the world. Satan is the ruler here. Everyone obeys his orders. The rulers get the saints killed. Scholars and priests do not behave like that. There is nothing in this world except crying for good people. The pot of sin is full and it is about to burst. Only after this it is the turn of the kingdom of God. This kingdom will arise like a sudden event and humanity will be reborn.

,

Jesus considered the scriptures of the Jews to be authentic, but he did not just interpret them like the scribes, but also dared to refine their rules. In the Sermon on the Mount, he said that I have not come to abolish the law of Moses and the teachings of the prophets, but to fulfill them.

Jesus gradually revealed, "I am the Christ, the Son of God. I have come from heaven to establish the kingdom of heaven." This aroused opposition from the Jewish leaders and they were accused of heresy. Roman governor Pontius He was hanged on the cross outside the north-west gate of Jerusalem in April 30 AD by Pilate's Hoom. Three days later, Jesus came back to life. The resurrection of Jesus gave courage to his followers and they celebrated the world. began to preach the kingdom of God to the people. The crucifixion of Christ is mentioned in the Qur'an only in a symbolic form in Surah An-Nisa. Thus, although they neither killed him nor crucified him, they (4:158) They were not aware of this deception. Indeed they did not kill Christ, but Allah took him to himself and crucified another person who looked like Christ. (Surah 4:58). In Quran Sharif, Christ said, 'Undoubtedly Allah is my Lord as well as your Lord', so his Worship this is the fair way (Surah: 3:31) |

Miracles of Hazrat Isa- 'When God said, Mary's son Isa remembering my blessings on you and mother, when we helped you by the Holy Spirit, then, you used to talk to humans in the lap and in a big state and we have given you the divine book Taught Torah and Injil, when you used to make the form of a bird out of clay and blow into it, it would become a living bird by my command. You used to heal the blind from birth and lepers by my order, you used to bring out the dead (by making alive) by my order. When you came to them with the evidence and We stopped the children of Israel from you, the disbelievers among them said that this is open magic. (5152).

Life introduction of Hazrat Musa (A)-(Judaism)

Hazrat Musa (Mozes) was born around 1350 BC in Egypt. His parents were Israelis and in those days the pharaohs had ordered the killing of all Israeli newborns and only the intervention of the pharaoh's daughter saved Moses' life. He studied theology in Heliopolis. He was deeply saddened by the atrocities on the Israelis in Egypt. To protect one of his caste brothers, Moses killed an Egyptian and went into hiding in an Arabian desert where he practiced austere practices believing that God had appointed him as the leader of the Jewish race to free it from Egyptian slavery. ordered. Organized his supporters and returned to Egypt during the reign of Moses II and repeatedly prayed that the caste brothers should be allowed to leave Egypt and return to Palestine, but their request was not accepted. ,

According to the story written in the Old Testament, 10 great plagues came on Egypt one after the other and they were allowed to leave the country considering them as the curse of Moses. Moses (Moses) said that his Nusa started towards Palestine with his followers. Had to cross the dreaded Sinai Desert on the way. This journey took 40 years and Moses did not live to complete the journey. On the way he preached simple ethics to his followers and it is believed that these instructions were received from God. these only Ten Commandments are called, which are still considered the basic principles of Christians in the world. Moses won over the magicians of Pharaoh with his miracles. At night he sent the children of Israel to their country. Seeing his slaves getting out of hand like this, Pharaoh ran after him with his army. All of them drowned there. On the way, the children of Israel used to get food from God - Manna, Salwa. When he went to talk to God and take his orders, the children of Israel were in charge of his brother Aaron. So here people started worshiping by making a calf by the mischief of the Samaritan. When Moses got angry, 'Aaron' said from behind - O son of my mother. Neither hold my beard nor my head.

I am afraid that you will say that you have created division in the children of Israel. The dust of Gabriel had created the power of speech by the Samaritan. (30-3-5)

When Moses went to talk to God, he asked for a vision. God said - you will not be able to see. Well, looking at the mountain, seeing that glory, he fell unconscious. God wrote his order on the plates and gave it to him. (7:16:18). Musa died around 13th century BC. The western part of the mountain is the valley where the Taurat was given to Hazrat Musa.

(Surah 28:44) The Tuba Valley is probably where Hazrat Musa saw the fire and Allah Ta'ala called him. Sina Island is situated at a distance of about 70 Km from the jungles.

There is a church here which is famous by the name of St. Kanthraton, there is a mosque which was built by Sultan Salim. "And the woman became pregnant and gave birth to a son, and seeing that the child was beautiful, she hid him for three months" (Exodus 2:2). Moses' mother was instructed in the form of Vahay to put the child in a box and leave it in the river and the river was ordered to put the box on the shore. So the mother of baby Moses did the same thing in the ark. That ark was placed on the shore at such a place where Pharaoh was present with his wife. He got the box lifted by his man. In this way Moses reached the person who was the enemy of God as well as himself. (Surah Taha, verse 39). On his way back from Madayan, he was not able to find his way in the desert of Sina, that suddenly he saw a fire. There is some way to know. When Hazrat Musa reached near the fire, Allah called out to him, 'I am your Lord.' Granted the respect of (mutual conversation). Be clear that Allah Ta'ala is pure from such things that it can be incorporated into a material object which is His own creation. Therefore the fire What appeared to Musa Alaihissalam was neither God nor God was absorbed in him, but it was a special kind of light which attracted Musa Alaihissalam towards itself.

They did hear the call of Allah and His words but they did not see Allah and the Qur'an confirms that later when Musa (peace be upon him) was called to give Shari'ah to Mount Tur, they made this request to Allah Ta ' ala That he should show his power to them. On his request, Allah Ta ' ala had said, "Lantrani means 'you will never be able to see me. " (Surah Aaraf 143).

Balamaibaar - a speech proven Jewish saint, because of whose curse Hazrat Musa Alaihissalam wandered in the forests for forty years, Baur' - was his father. ,

Life introduction of Guru Nanak-(Sikhism)

Guru Nanak was born in Nankana Sahib (Talwandi) on April 15, 1469 AD. At the age of 15, he was given education of Punjabi, Hindi, Farsi and culture. He was a very intelligent and calm person. He was married to Sulakshana Devi at the age of 18. The places through which Guru Nanak had passed have taken the form of pilgrimage today. Guru Nanak left home in a way to spread his principles and started teaching people the lessons of truth and love. He fiercely opposed the then superstitions, hypocrisy etc. by roaming around the place. He was a strong supporter of Hindu Muslim unity. To establish religious harmony, he visited all the pilgrimages and made people of all religions his disciples.

He established a new religion by blending the basic and best teachings of both Hinduism and Islam. Whose foundation was love and equality. This later came to be known as Sikhism. After burning his knowledge in India, he traveled to Mecca and Medina and the residents there were also very impressed by him. After traveling for 25 years, Nanak settled in Kartarpur and stayed there and started preaching. His speech is still preserved in the Guru Granth Sahib. He died in 1539 AD while reciting Jayuji.

Zarathustra's life introduction - (Parsi religion)

Zarathustra was born in 700 BC in a caste named Madia. He was born in a place called Usmiya in Azerbaijan, his real name was Ispitama. Greek scholars consider him 6000 years earlier than Plato, according to the Bible he was born in 0 BC, according to Iranian legends, this poet was under the patronage of a king named Vistasp. William Jackson considers it to be 660 AD and Bill Duro considers it to be 6th century AD. His father's name was Pomashashpa and mother's name was Durodha, but according to Meyer, it is not appropriate to consider it as 6th century AD. Presenting (1) The religion of Zarathustra had become very popular in every Vamshi reign, so it should be considered before the rule (2) Asurbanipal whose time is believed to be before the seventh century AD, in an article Asar Bhajan along with Igigio and opposing it There is a description of ghost souls with which seems to be the influence of Zoroastrian religion. This description is of none other than Ahuramazda along with Ameshspento and 7 gods. It is said that many good horses are found in his kingdom, which he has the right because of the grace of Ahuramazda, it is clear that the religion of Zoroastrianism was prevalent before the seventh century AD. (4) King Darius I from us describes himself as a worshiper of Ahumazda in one of his inscriptions (5) Harvamsi Naresho The religion mentioned in the reign appears to be a developed form of the

Zoroastrian religion. The language of the Harvamshi inscriptions is very different from that of Zoreaster's Gathas. According to linguists, the language of Zoreaster's legends is about 500 years older than the language of Harvamsi inscriptions, yet most of the scholars consider Zorester's period to be before 600 AD. Zarathustra was very intelligent and very thoughtful, who after getting education at the age of 15, abandoned the world at the age of 20 and started living in Mount Kandraao for deep study of worldly and transcendental subjects. Divine powers obstructed his work but he was not deterred by them. At the age of 30, he attained enlightenment on Mount Sablan. It is said that when he was sitting on the bank of a river called Avetak, an angel appeared and took him to Ahuramazda and Ahuramazda gave him the Avesta and told him to preach it. Ahuramazda sent his angels to Vistasp to accept Zoreaster as his teacher and to live for 125 years. Zorester married three times after making Vistaspa his disciple. Meanwhile, the neighboring Sandhu attacked Vistasap. The Turani tribes of Asia attacked Iran only after seeing such a great progress of the religion of poet Zorester. Some scholars are of the opinion that Zorester was killed in the second religious war against him. He was 75 years old when he died. Zorester's view was that life is a struggle between the forces of good and evil. Ahura Mazda is the Spirit of Good and Mithas, the Light, is his helper. The spirit of evil is the henchman of every Angramanyu or Ahriman lie. Man cannot remain neutral in this struggle. He has to fight for the truth and to lead a virtuous life. Zarathustra was very firm on the view that tradition (like stagnant water) is static while knowledge is always moving forward.

Zorester resolved to be his own teacher and to learn by personal observation and deep thought. He thought that life is not only woven with threads of joy and happiness, it also has a fair amount of worries and sorrows mixed in it. Zarathustra was religious at heart but his daily experience of the religion that was practiced and followed around him and the religious beliefs of the ancestors caused him to turn away. The sight of the temples smelling of the blood of sacrificed animals gave him goosebumps, so he found that in the name of religion, fruitless orthodoxy, hypocrisy, religious fanaticism, cowardly mutilation, superstitious birth fear and ostentatious piety were being displayed. Hence Zarathustra lost his faith in his religion.

Gautama (life introduction of Mahatma Buddha - (Buddhism or Dhamma)

Mahatma Buddha was born in 563 AD in the Lumbini forest near Kapilvastu, the capital of Shakyas (present day Rummindei). His mother's name was Maya Devi. Siddhartha's mother Prajapati Gautami nurtured him after his mother Maya Devi died due to childbirth. Perhaps this is the reason why he is also called Gautama. Terai of Nepal, he was the son of King Shuddhodhan. Since childhood Signs of detachment and kindness began to appear in Gautam. Seeing his son's deep indifference towards worldly life, King Shuddhodhan married him at the age of 16 to a beautiful princess named Yashodhara. Decorated with alluring and attractive materials and facilities and full of luxury. These facilities also could not calm the distraught heart of Virakat Bhautam. A son named Rahul was also born. The scenes of old age, sickness and death showed his indifference towards the world and It is good for them to live in solitude by giving up lust etc. Began to feel The result was that at the age of 29, at night, he left his palace and royal splendor to search for the truth. His planetary renunciation is called Mahabhinishkraman. He continued to live the life of a monk for 6 consecutive years. During this he studied in the hermitage of two Brahmin teachers. Even after this, his curiosity was not satisfied and he was not satisfied, then he did severe penance in the dense forest and tortured his body. But failed.

The body dried up and became skeletal. At last he gave up the ascetic life, stopped torturing the body and took a bath in the Niranjana river and sat on a seat of grass under a Peepal tree in present-day Bodh Gaya. There he suddenly saw the truth. His inner mind became enlightened with the knowledge of Brahma that great peace is in his heart only. That is what they should search for. This is called great wisdom. Since then he was called Buddhist or Tathagat. After this he went to Rishipattan of Sarnath near Banaras. There he gave his first religious sermon, as a result of which five persons became his disciples. King Kaushal Prasenjit and King Bimbasar of Magadha and an unknown enemy accepted his principles and became his disciples. After 45 years of continuous preaching, he died (Nirvana) in 487 AD in the capital of Malla Republic (present Kasia, district Deoria, U.P.). This event is called Mahaparinirvan in Buddhist literature.

The Buddha once told the Mahashreshti, Anayapindaka, his most devoted householder disciple, who had established for him the famous Jetavana Bihar at Savatthi (Awasti), that the householder who leads a simple family life can enjoy four types of happiness. are obtained. The first happiness is economic security or the enjoyment of sufficient property acquired justly and properly (Asti Sukh). The third happiness is the happiness of being free from debt (Anan Sukh), the fourth happiness is the happiness of leading an innocent and pure life without doing evil through mind, speech and action (Anvajj Sukh). Shresthi (Mahajan) has been warned that the value of economic and material pleasures is not equal to even one-sixteenth part of the spiritual pleasure arising from a blameless and virtuous life.

Life of Barddhaman Mahavira - (Jainism)

Various views regarding the date of birth of the founder of the religion are as follows (1) Mahavira was born about 600 years before Christ in Kurugram near Vaishali located in Muzaffarpur district under Bihar. happened . (History of the ancient civilizations of the world). (2) He was born in Kundalpur city of Bihar province in 599 AD. (World famous religions, sects and sects). 2001). (3) Mahavira was born around 540 BC in a village near Vaishali (Bihar). (Chronicle Year Book 2001) According to Jain legends, Mahavira was born in the beginning of the 6th century BC. The actual dates of his death and his demise are controversial. He is also called the one who conquers the senses. Prince Vardhaman had practiced all the arts of the Kshatriyas till his youth. On the insistence of his mother, he also married Yashoda Devi, the daughter of King Samasveer, who gave birth to a girl child, Priyadarshana. But the life of a householder seemed to him to be a bondage, an illusion, from which his soul used to shake to get rid of it. When Prince Vardhaman was 28 years old, his desire to leave his home and become a monk still did not subside, but on the insistence of brother Nandivdhan, he had to stay at home for two more years. At the age of 30, leaving home, the present took Diksha. As soon as he took Diksha, he attained manah paryaya jnana (the power to know the mind of others). To achieve complete victory over the senses and the mind, he did severe penance for twelve and a half years. During this, sometimes for six months, he He used to observe waterless fast, sometimes for months standing and meditating, he had to bear severe hardships during penance. A cowherd hit a nail in his ear. Snakes, scorpions and other animals gave them terrible troubles. Storm, rain, heat and hail all tried their best to disturb him but he remained unmoved like a mountain. Seeing this patience and morale, Indra called him 'Mahavir'. At last the penance was completed and Mahavir became free from all desires and lusts and became a benevolent, omniscient and great master. In major cities like Rajagriha, Sravastishali, Mahavir did Chaturmasya (preaching the same religion for four months). He attained nirvana at Pavapuri (near Patna) on Kartik Amavasya in 527 AD at the age of 72. From this year the Veer Nirvana Samvat of Jains begins. Siddhartha was the father of Mahavira, the leader of the republic of the Gyatrik-dynasty in Kundagrama. His mother's name was Trishala, who was the sister of Chetak, the leader of the Vaishali republic. His childhood name was Vardhaman. He always used to preach religion in Digambar state without clothes.

Mahavira rejected the authenticity and supremacy of the Vedas. His thoughts were quite logical and judicious, the knowledge of the truth of intellectual dogma is partial. Therefore, it is wrong to declare other's views as untrue. In Jainism, this principle is famous by the name of Syahvada.

The founder of Taoism

Lao Tzu was born in China around the 6th century BC. Lao Tzu compiled his teachings in a book called Tao Te Ching (Tao Te Ching). The Three Gems of Taoism are kindness, self-control and humility. Lao Tzu taught to do good in return of evil. Lao Tzu's disciples used the Tao Teh Qing as a source of miracles, and Taoism was reduced to mere rituals 10 BC By the middle of the 2nd century, Taoism had become so corrupted that it started worshiping Lao Tzu as a deity. Gave .

The founder of the Baha'i religion

The founder of the Baha'i religion was Mirza Hussain Ali.——whose nickname was Baha'u'llah (glory of God's light). He was born on November 12, 1817 in a place called Majindran, Iran. He became famous by the name of Bab, which means Door, and at the age of 25, he claimed to be such a messenger in May 1844. Whose purpose was to incarnate. In July 1850, when he was killed by a firing squad in the public square of Tabrez Nagar, this religion inspires a custom of marriage, good character and decency in family life and calls divorce as bad. God is one and humanity (also) is one and the only religion of the prophets of the incarnations is love and unity." Every religion is true, beautiful and authentic. It is a message from God for the age when it appears.

德侔天地 道冠古今
刪述六經 垂憲萬世

Confucianism

The word originated from the name of Confucius (Kung Fu Su) 551-479 BC, the most important and revered person in Chinese history. Since childhood, he had a longing for knowledge. In his youth, he had the opportunity to meet Lao Tzu and exchange views with him. Lao Tzu was a famous person in those days. Struggling in poverty, Confucius first held the position of an ordinary government employee but later he reached the position of magistrate of the state. Other people started getting jealous of his efficient rule, by conspiring they got him fired from the job in 0496 AD. After that he wandered here and there in a homeless and torn condition and finally he died in 0478 BC at the age of 73. Khand Phoolju (our lord Khug) was born in Gang Kul in 551 AD. After his death, his teachings were compiled in the form of a collection of aphorisms. Confucius was given respect like China. To be honest, Confucius was not the founder of religion, but a virtuous moralist. He preserved the ancient teachings of China, systematized them and preached them to the people.

Idiol of Hinduism

Acharya Gaunapada (Birth – around 800 years BC)

Acharya Gaunapada, who established the principle of monism, has a dispute about both the date of birth and the place of birth, but it is true that he belongs to the period after the famous Buddhist philosopher Acharya Nagarjuna and Acharya Nagarjuna's lifetime was 401 years BC. is believed to belong to. Gaunapada's teacher was Shukdevacharya. Gaunapada has written commentaries on Mandukyakarika and Sankhyakarika on Mandukya Upanishad. There are a total of four episodes in Gaunapada's Mandukyakarika. The name of the first episode is 'Agam' episode. In this there is an explanation of the four states of the soul or consciousness. The name of the second episode is 'Baitathya' episode, in which the futility of the world is rendered. The name of the third episode is 'Advaita'. It describes Asparsha Yoga. The name of the fourth episode is 'Alat'. In this the world has been compared to Alatchakra or Agnichakra. Due to this analogy, some people also call Gaunapada as 'disguised Buddhist'. Gaunapadas do a subtle parapsychological analysis of the soul or conscious element. They believe that the soul has different states like Vishwa, Tejas and Pragya, not different forms. They prove from the explanation of the waking, dream, deep sleep and turiya states of consciousness that the Self is a form. The soul is non dual form. This Self is realized only after the retirement of ignorance. After self-knowledge, the whole world is retired. Duality gets destroyed. Brahman is calm and non-dual element. Casteism is his main principle. Paramarth elements are unknown. There is one eternal, one form, one juice and three times. Nothing is produced. There is no difference of any kind. Gaunapada propounds the main principles of monism in Mandukyakarika. Such as the sequence of real existence, the unity of Brahman and Atman, Maya, knowledge or knowledge being the direct means of salvation, absolute zero being inconceivable.

Propounded theory: Advaitaism. Text '- Commentary on Mandukyakarika Sankhyakarika with four episodes 'Agam', 'Baitathya', 'Advaita' and 'Alat'.

Adi Shankara (Born 509 BC Died 477 BC)

Shankar's philosophy is actually a philosophy of subtle rationality. Shankara has given the principle of monism in the Vedantic tradition. Where Shankar had full authority over extremely rigorous logic, on the other hand he had an equal interference in excellent poetry. Shankar was born in Kaldi village of Kerala. In his childhood he entered the Vedic school run by Govindapada, a disciple of Advaitacharya Gaunapada. It is said that he had memorized all the Vedas at the age of only eight. Researchers consider his birth to be in the eighth century, but scholars of many religious groups believe him to be even earlier. Shankara was not just a Vitarag Parivrajak. As an Acharya, he toured India and interacted with scholars of different schools of thought. Shankara in his book 'Brahmagyanavali' Expressing the essence of his monistic opinion in 'Mala', he writes in half a verse that 'Brahma Satyam Jaganmithya Jeevo Brahmaiva Na Parah' means only Brahman is true, this world full of diversity is false and in Ashram analysis the living beings are not different from Brahman. . Shankar is of the firm opinion that the truth from the elemental point of view is that only that element is Sat, which exists uninterruptedly in all the three times past, present and future. Such ultimate truth is Sachchidananda Brahma. It is such a supreme being, which, being uninterrupted in all three times, enjoys its own bliss in its consciousness. Some people do not understand the essence of Shankar's concept that the world is false and accuse him of world prohibition, but these people probably do not understand or recognize the philosophical meaning of Shankar's three-dimensional power. Those who attack Shankar and say that he ignores the reality of the world, they forget that the Acharya not only believes in the practical existence of the world, but also declares that there is no negation of the world without self-realization. Happen . Siddhanta Advaita.

Books - 'Physical commentary', 'Gita commentary', 'Mandukyakarika', 'Dashopanishad', 'Vivek', 'Chudamani', 'Saundarya Lahari' and 'Self-realization'.
References- An introduction to Islam, 101 personalities, those other texts, etc.

Hamza ibn Ali ibn Ahmad (Druze Ṣurūz) Founder of the religion

Hamza ibn Ali ibn Ahmad. 985–c. 1021) was an 11th-century Persian Isma'ili missionary and the founding leader of the Druze. He was born in Zozan, Greater Khorasan in Samanid-ruled Persia (modern Khaf, Razavi Khorasan Province, Iran), and preached his heretical side of Isma'ilism in Cairo during the reign of the Fatimid caliph al-Hakim bi-Amr Allah. According to Hamza, al-Hakim was the manifest manifestation of God. Despite opposition from the established Isma'ili clergy, Hamza persevered, was apparently tolerated or even patronized by al-Hakim, and established a parallel hierarchy of missionaries in Egypt and Syria. After al-Hakim's disappearance in February 1021 – or, most likely, murder – Hamza and his followers were persecuted by the new regime. Hamza himself announced his retirement in his last letter to his followers, in which he also promised that al-Hakim would soon return and usher in the end times. Hamza disappeared after that, although a contemporary source claims that he fled to Mecca, where he was recognized and executed. His disciple Baha al-Din al-Muqtana resumed Hamza's missionary effort in 1027–1042, finalizing the tenets of the Druze religion.

The Druze durūz),

who call themselves al-Muwahidun (literally 'the monotheists' or 'the unifiers') are an Arab and Arabic-speaking esoteric ethno-religious group from West Asia who follow the Druze faith, an Abrahamic, monotheistic, syncretic and ethnoreligious religion whose main tenets emphasize the unity of God, reincarnation, and the eternity of the soul. Most Druze religious practices are kept secret. The Druze do not allow outsiders to convert to their religion. Marriage outside the Druze religion is rare and strongly discouraged. The Druze retain the Arabic language and culture as an integral part of their identity, and Arabic is their primary language.

The Epistles of Wisdom is the foundational and central text of the Druze religion. The Druze religion originated in Ismailism (a branch of Shia Islam), and was influenced by Christianity, Gnosticism, Neoplatonism, Zoroastrianism, Gandhara Buddhism, Manichaeism, Pythagoreanism, and other philosophies and beliefs, producing a distinct and secretive theology based on esoteric interpretation of scripture, which emphasizes the role of the mind and truth. The Druze believe in theodicy and reincarnation.

The Druze believe that at the end of the cycle of reincarnation, which is achieved through successive rebirths, the soul is united with the cosmic mind (al-'aql al-kulli).

The Druze have a special reverence for Shu'aib, whom they believe to be the same person as the Biblical Jethro. The Druze believe that Adam, Noah, Abraham, Moses, Jesus, Muhammad, and the Ismaili Imam Muhammad ibn Ismail were prophets. Druze tradition also honors and reveres Salman the Persian, al-Khidr (whom they identify as Elijah, reincarnated as John the Baptist and St. George), Job, Luke the Evangelist, and others as "masters" and "prophets".

Even though the faith originally developed from Ismailism, the Druze are not Muslims. The Druze faith is one of the major religious groups in the Levant, with 800,000 to one million followers. They are found mainly in Lebanon, Syria, and Israel, with smaller communities in Jordan. They make up 5.5% of the population of Lebanon, 3% of Syria, and 1.6% of Israel. The oldest and most densely populated Druze communities exist around Jabal al-Druze (literally "Mountain of the Druze") in Mount Lebanon and the south of Syria.

The Druze community played an important role in shaping the history of the Levant, where it plays an important political role. As a religious minority in every country where they are found, they have often faced persecution by various Muslim regimes, including contemporary Islamic extremism.

God

The Druze concept of deity is declared by them to be one of strict and uncompromising unity. The main Druze doctrine states that God is both transcendental and immanent, in that He is above all attributes, but at the same time, He is also present.

In their desire to maintain a strict confession of unity, they stripped God of all attributes (tanzih). In God, there is no attribute separate from His essence. He is wise, powerful, and just, not by wisdom, power, and justice, but by His essence. God is the "whole of existence", not "above existence" or on His throne, which makes Him "limited". There is neither "how", "when", nor "where" about Him; He is beyond comprehension.

In this dogma they are akin to the quasi-philosophical, quasi-religious body that flourished under al-Mamun and was known as the Mu'tazila and the Fraternal Order of the Brethren of Purity (Ikhwan al-Safa).

Unlike the Mu'tazila, and similar to some branches of Sufism, the Druze believe in the concept of tajalli (meaning "divine appearance"). Tajalli is often misunderstood by scholars and writers and is commonly confused with the concept of the Avatar. [Avatar] is the core spiritual belief in the Druze and certain other intellectual and spiritual traditions ... In a mystical sense, it refers to the light of God experienced by certain mystics who have reached a high level of purity in their spiritual journey. Thus, God is perceived as the Lahut [divine] who manifests his light in the station (maqam) of the Nasut [physical realm] without the Nasut becoming the Lahut. It is like one's image in a mirror: one is in the mirror, but does not become the mirror. The Druze manuscripts are emphatic and warn against the belief that the Nasut is God ... Neglecting this warning, individual seekers, scholars, and other onlookers have regarded al-Hakim and other figures as divine. ... Druze Approaches to ScriptureScriptures

Druze sacred texts include the Quran and the Letters of Wisdom. Other ancient Druze writings include the Rasa'il al-Hind (Letters of India) and previously lost (or hidden) manuscripts such as al-Munfarid bi-Dhatihi and al-Shari'a al-Ruhaniyya, as well as didactic and controversial texts.

Reincarnation

Reincarnation is a paramount principle in the Druze faith. Reincarnation occurs immediately after one's death because there is an eternal duality of body and soul and it is impossible for the soul to exist without a body. A human soul will only transmigrate into a human body, unlike Neoplatonic, Hindu and Buddhist belief systems according to which the soul can transmigrate into any living being. Furthermore, a male Druze can only be reborn as another male Druze and a female Druze can only be reborn as another female Druze. A Druze cannot be reborn into the body of a non-Druze. Additionally, souls cannot be divided and the number of souls that exist in the universe is finite. The cycle of reincarnation is continuous and the only way to escape is to be continually reborn. When this happens, the soul becomes one with the cosmic mind and achieves ultimate happiness. The Time Guardian Treaty

The Time Guardian Treaty (myth Wali al-Zaman) is considered the gateway to the Druze religion, and they believe that all Druze in their past lives have signed this charter, and the Druze believe that this charter binds with human souls after death.I trust in our Maula al-Hakim, the One God, the Individual, the Eternal, who is beyond joints and numbers, the son of (someone) who has approved recognition on himself and on his soul, on his mind and body being sound, avoiding permissiveness, obedient and not compelled, rejecting all creeds, writings and all religions and beliefs on varieties of differences, and he knows nothing except obedience to the Almighty Maula al-Hakim, and obedience is worship and it does not consist in worship that ever one attended or waited for, and he entrusted his soul and his body and his money and everything that he had to the Almighty Maula al-Hakim.   [clarification needed]Esotericism

The Druze believe that many of the teachings given by prophets, religious leaders and sacred books have esoteric meanings preserved for people of wisdom, with some teachings being symbolic and allegorical in nature, and divide the understanding of sacred books and teachings into three layers.

According to the Druze, these layers are as follows:

The explicit or esoteric (zahir), accessible to anyone who can read or hear;

The hidden or esoteric (batin), which is accessible to those who are willing to explore and learn through the concept of interpretation;

And the hidden within the hidden, a concept known as the anagoge, which is inaccessible to all except for a few truly enlightened individuals who truly understand the nature of the universe.

The Druze do not believe that the esoteric meaning supersedes or necessarily eliminates the exoteric meaning. Hamza bin Ali refutes such claims, stating that if the esoteric interpretation of taharah (purity) is purity of the heart and soul, this does not mean that one can abandon one's bodily purity, because if a person lies in his speech then namaz (prayer) is worthless and that the esoteric and exoteric meanings complement each other.

Joseph Smith, founder of the Church of Jesus Christ of Latter-day Saints.

Joseph Smith (born December 23, 1805, Sharon, Vermont, U.S.—died June 27, 1844, Carthage, Illinois) was an American prophet and founder of the Church of Jesus Christ of Latter-day Saints.

Smith came from an unremarkable New England family. His grandfather, Asael Smith, lost most of his property in Topsfield, Massachusetts, during the economic downturn of the 1780s and eventually moved to Vermont, where Smith's father, Joseph Smith, Sr., established himself as a farmer. After the birth of Joseph Smith, Jr., a series of crop failures forced the family to move to Palmyra, New York. His mother, Lucy Mack, came from a Connecticut family that had disengaged from conventional Congregationalism and leaned toward Seekerism, a movement that looked for a new revelation to restore true Christianity. Although privately religious, the family rarely attended church, and after they moved to Palmyra they became involved in magic and treasure-seeking. Lucy Smith attended Presbyterian meetings, but her husband refused to accompany her, and Joseph, Jr., remained at home with his father.

Religious differences within the family and over religious revivals in the Palmyra area left Smith perplexed about where to find a church. When he was 14, he prayed for help, and, according to his own account, God and Jesus appeared to him. In answer to his question about which was the right church, they told him that all the churches were wrong. Although a local minister to whom he related the vision dismissed it as a delusion, Smith continued to believe in its authenticity. In 1823 he received another revelation: while praying for forgiveness, he later reported, an angel calling himself Moroni appeared in his bedroom and told him about a set of golden plates containing a record of the ancient inhabitants of America. Smith found the plates buried in a stone box not far from his father's farm. Four years later, the angel permitted him to remove the plates and instructed him to translate the characters engraved on their surfaces with the aid of special stones called "interpreters." Smith insisted that he did not compose the book but merely "translated" it under divine guidance. Completing the work in less than 90 days, he published it in March 1830 as a 588-page volume called the Book of Mormon.

The Book of Mormon told the 1,000-year history of the Israelites, who were led from Jerusalem to a promised land in the Western Hemisphere. In their new home, they built a civilization, fought wars, heard the word of prophets, and received a visit from Christ after his resurrection. The book resembled the Bible in its length and complexity and in its division into books named for individual prophets. According to the book itself, one of the prophets, a general named Mormon, abridged and assembled the records of his people, engraving the history on gold plates. Later, about 400 ce, the record keepers, known as Nephites, were wiped out by their enemies, the Lamanites, presumably the ancestors of the American Indians

Martin Luther

Martin Luther was born on November 10, 1483 and, as was the tradition them, was baptized as soon as possible so that if he died his soul would go to heaven. Luther's father rose from a lowly copper miner into a self-made mining and smelting entrepreneur and town councilor. Martin began Latin school when he was seven and graduated from Erfurt University with a bachelor's degree at the age of 21 after attending for only 18 months. He went on to get his masters degree but disappointed his father when he chose to attend an Augustinian monastery intend of pursuing a career as a lawyer.

Luther changed his mind about his legal career at the age of 21 when, he said, a lightning bolt hurled him to the ground during a violent thunderstorm."Walled around with terror and agony of sudden death," Luther wrote. He shouted, "Help, St. Anne! I will be a monk." He survived the event and entered a monastery. St. Anne, the patron saint of miners, was no doubt a religious figure that he felt particularly close to because of his father.

Luther visited Rome when he was 27. To get there he walked over the Alps and covered the entire 800 miles distance from Erfurt by foot in 40 days. In Rome he wrote he ran around like "a mad saint through all the churches and crypts."

During his early thirties Luther was elected as a vicar of monasteries throughout the Saxony region. His duties included collecting rents, mediating over monastic disputes, preaching, lecturing on theology at the university and supervising the studies of fledgling friars. Because these chores were time consuming he skipped meals, slept less and prayed all day Saturday to fulfill his seven daily canonical hours of prayer. In 1512 he was appointed a professor of biblical studies at the University of Wittenberg and also worked as a parish priest in the town of Wittenberg.

Luther, consumed by guilt and paralyzed by fear that his merit was not enough, concluded that man was not worthy of God's forgiveness that God might or might not grant, only through his grace. Luther believed the devil took up residence in his body from time to time and occasionally had visions of the devil spinning in his head and roaring in his ear. Some scholars believed his problem was Meniere's disease, which attacks the middle ear. Martin Luther is crediting with inventing the game of nine pins.

Luther believed

Luther believed that faith led to salvation. Rituals, good works and mediation by the clergy in comparison were not important. He criticized the pope, celibacy and other rules and recommended that individuals study the Bible rather than having it delivered to them by clergymen. Luther said man can work towards salvation through penances, pardons and pilgrimages but only through faith that Christ died for mankind's sins on the cross and that faith was freely given with the trust of the word of God. He said also that more could be achieved through prayer and good works than by armed revolt pushed by the fanatic religious cults of his time and expensive indulgences of the Catholic church. The Lutheran is motto "By grace alone; through faith alone."

Luther asserted that humankind did not need the corrupt Catholic church to mediate between humankind and God. He believed that Christians should be governed by temporal rulers in their own land not by the Pope. He called for the abolition of the papacy and asserted that every Christian could be his or her own priest. Luther based his positions on St. Paul's Letter to the Romans. "Works" Paul said had no bearing on the afterlife." When he was asked if being one with God was based on "the principle of works." Paul said no.

The purpose of Martin Luther's efforts was to give lay people access the Bible, the church and redemption. Luther believed that the Bible should be read by everyone not just the clergy and promoted literacy, education and making scriptures understandable to ordinary people. Luther is famous for highlighting the importance of a direct relationship between god and the individual without a clergy and translating the bible in into everyday language of the people. He did not intend to displace the Catholic religion, only to reform it, and he was appalled by the development of the Lutheran church.

My another books

Sr no.	Book
1	World's Major religions, doctrines and sects
2	An introduction to the Holy Qur'an and it's unsolved mysteries
3	How did humans and language originate ?
4	Islam an introduction and sect
5	Sermons of great people
6	Prayer
7	Allah an introduction
8	Is Al khizr still alive today?
9	Story of harut and marut
10	Grief
11	The mysterious story of Al kahf (Ar raqim)
12	Naming of God
13	Who was Sheeba?
14	Death concept of the Holy Quran

15	What is soul? In view of Religion and science
16	Real Alexander Zulqurnain
17	Where is peace?
18	Origin of ancient religious book, it's author and original copy
19	An introduction to the bible and is the original bible still available today?
20	Does a parallel universe exist?
21	Promise to your self or God?
22	Evidence of God existance
23	Prediction of holy Quran
24	Humanity in the holy Quran?
25	Commandnends of the holy Quran,right or wrong?
26	Similarity in the world famous holy books
27	Is Zulkifl the same Gautam Buddha?
28	Adam to Muhammad
29	Why isolated?

30	For Divorce! Who is responsible?
31	Hadith to denomination
32	Karma is the best?
33	According to dreams, religion and Science
34	End day

<u>All these books are available in Hindi</u> language and other international languages and are also available in e-book for <u>free on Google Play Store</u>.

All the books are available in paper back edition and hard cover edition as well.

These books are also available on Amazon,Flipkart and notionpress.com.

My personal introduction

My name is Abdul Waheed, my father's name is Late Haji Ubaidur Rahman and mother's name is Jaibunnisa. I have liked scientific ideology since childhood and have a calm nature and attachment to books. Due to which my curiosity interest has been continuously used in new discoveries and information. I got selected in polytechnic while doing BSc, but unfortunately it remained incomplete because father and brother died.

Two words of my father, which are very precious for my life,

<u>first - earn honestly, do not take support of lies,</u>

<u>secondly, respect food and eat as much as you want</u>. That's why the education remained incomplete due to the responsibility of the house, then later getting married. Still did not lose courage and today the book is available in front of you in the form of my thoughts. If any information is left incomplete, please let us know. ,

Thank you .
Contact-
Abdul Waheed, Barabanki, Uttar Pradesh, India
https://www.facebook.com/profile.php?id=100091298026218